Miss Bridges

Sir Thomas Maxwell and his Ward

Miss Bridges

Sir Thomas Maxwell and his Ward

Reprint of the original, first published in 1875.

1st Edition 2024 | ISBN: 978-3-38525-143-4

Verlag (Publisher): Outlook Verlag GmbH, Zeilweg 44, 60439 Frankfurt, Deutschland
Vertretungsberechtigt (Authorized to represent): E. Roepke, Zeilweg 44, 60439 Frankfurt, Deutschland
Druck (Print): Books on Demand GmbH, In de Tarpen 42, 22848 Norderstedt, Deutschland

SIR THOMAS MAXWELL

AND

HIS WARD.

BY

MISS BRIDGES.

LONDON:

R. WASHBOURNE, 18 PATERNOSTER ROW.

1875.

To my Cousin

EDWARD KNOTTESFORD FORTESCUE, ESQ.,

WHOSE TALENTS ADORN, AND WHOSE

CHRISTIAN VIRTUES

CONSECRATE HIS HOME,

This Work

IS GRATEFULLY AND AFFECTIONATELY INSCRIBED

BY

THE AUTHOR.

SIR THOMAS MAXWELL

AND

HIS WARD.

CHAPTER I.

> " My hair is grey, but not with years,
>   Nor grew it white,
>   In a single night,
> As men's have grown from sudden fears."
>
> BYRON.

" NOT at home—say I am not at home," said a young lady to the footman, who presented a card on a silver salver.

" The gentleman is here, miss," was the reply. And true enough, there entered the library at that moment a man of distinguished appearance, about fifty years of age, whose hair of snowy whiteness threw out the force of a pair of very dark eyes with singular effect. A deep flush suffused the cheeks of the girl; she rose from her chair, threw down her novel, bowed coldly, and turned a glance of something like defiance on the intruder.

"I was not prepared for such a reception from you, my child!" said Father Cuthbert with calm dignity.

"But I asked you not to come and see me," said the girl, pushing her braids of raven hair in an excited way from her temples. "You ought not to have come," she added, though her ladylike instinct compelled her to make a sign to the Priest to be seated.

"And why should I not come to see you?" he asked; "I have not forgotten the little girl who made her first confession to me."

Jane dashed a tear from her eye, and exclaimed, "But I have grown wicked since then, and the world has spoiled me."

"I dare say it has—that world which you

never ought to have entered. You were happy, my child, in the holy shade of the cloister."

"Don't speak of it, or I shall go mad. I must drown all memory of the past in present amusement," and she tried to laugh, though there was a hollow ring in her mirth. "Don't I look happy?" she continued; "look at my last photo," and she showed him a likeness of herself in ball costume.

"I would not have looked at you, if I had seen you in such a dress," was his grave rebuke.

"I knew it," she said; "I wanted to shock you. You see now, there can be nothing in common between us. I have chosen my path, which goes the opposite way to yours."

"The Good Shepherd went out of His path to bring back a stray sheep, and I shall do the same for you."

"Pray save yourself the trouble; it is too late in the day. I have gone through an ordeal which you have little idea of."

"And therefore I want you to tell me all about it. I know that you have been sorely tried. You will feel better when you have told me everything."

And he fixed those powerful eyes upon her, which had so often subdued the proud spirit of her childhood. For a moment she wavered, and then she exclaimed passionately—"No, I won't—I don't believe in any one, or in anything good."

Father Cuthbert saw that he could do no more at present.

"You cannot prevent me from praying for you," he said, with grave sadness in his tone. He then bade her good-bye, and departed.

Jane walked restlessly up and down the room for some minutes, and then she took from her pocket a letter with a foreign post-mark, which she suddenly crushed in her hand, as the door opened, and a very lovely young lady entered the room. This was Charlotte, her eldest sister, though no one would have thought that the two girls were related. The colouring and the expression were so utterly unlike. There was a certain swan-like grace about Charlotte;

her complexion was pink and white, and her hazel eyes matched her golden brown hair. You could not say that her features were regular, but she had something more than beauty; you would have described her as a fascinating creature. Jane was taller than her sister; she was a brunette, and there was a world of passionate thought in her dark eyes.

"I am glad to hear that you have had a clerical visitor," said Miss Maxwell kindly. "You must have been glad to see your old friend Father Cuthbert again."

A sort of spasm passed over the features of the younger sister. She made no reply, but drawing Charlotte to the open window, led her out into the garden, and said—

"I want to talk to you about something else."

Charlotte was pained at this want of confidence, but made no remark. Presently her sister added—

"I want you to use your influence with the governor, to take us to Switzerland this summer.

If you were to express a wish, the thing would soon be settled."

"I thought you hadn't enjoyed yourself there last year with Aunt Edith. Instead of doing you good, it seemed to do you harm. You came back as pale as a sheet."

"Nevertheless I want to try the effect of the mountain breezes again."

At this moment the dressing-bell rang, and the two girls returned to the house. Soon after they made their appearance in the drawing-room in pretty dresses of mauve muslin. Sir Thomas Maxwell came in from the verandah, and as he gave his arm to Mrs. Blunt, his widowed sister, he turned for a moment to Jane, and said—

"I wish to speak to you, child, in the library after dinner."

"Very well, papa," was the young lady's answer.

Sir Thomas Maxwell was a grand-looking man, about forty-five. His dark hair was just touched with grey. His noble countenance expressed the highest intellect, and nowhere did his gifts shine forth more brightly than in the bosom of his family. He loved his daughters—he was proud of them; but he also ruled them. Charlotte adored her father with a blind, unquestioning worship. She had a spirit of her own, and sometimes came into collision with him; but she always gave way in the end. Jane, on the contrary, was jealous of his great love for her sister, and often opposed him on the most important points. Aunt Edith was a lady of the old school. She was Sir Thomas's half-sister, and had been brought up a Protestant by her mother. She was a sensible, conscientious woman, living up to the light she had, and making it a point of honour not to interfere with the religion of her nieces, to whom she had for many years filled the place of their lost parent. Agnes, the youngest daughter, was at a Convent school, and was approaching the term of her education, when she was to come home to Kensington.

CHAPTER II.

"Face to face in my chamber—my silent chamber I
        saw her—
God and she and I only—there I sat down, to draw
        her
Soul through the clefts of confession—speak, I am
        holding thee fast
As the Angel of Resurrection shall do it at the last."
                                                BROWNING.

IT was by no means with an easy mind
that Jane followed her father into the
library. He took his usual easy chair,
and kindly held out his hand for her to come
near him.

   " Dear child," he began, "you had a visit from
Father Cuthbert, to-day. I am sorry that I
missed seeing him. Had he anything important
to say ?"

"O dear no"—said the girl; "I can't think what made him come at all."

"Perhaps you had neglected your duty in going to see him."

Jane was silent; and when her father turned upon her the full gaze of his eagle eye, he read in her countenance an expression of obstinate sullenness.

His tone became somewhat severe, as he said, "I am responsible to God for my children, and their spiritual welfare. It has grieved me, Jane, that for many months past, nearly a year, I should think, I have seen no sign of your approaching the holy Sacraments. I have kept silence, and prayed for you in secret, as I did not wish to be premature in interfering with your conscience. But I can be silent no longer —and I require to know from you, my daughter, the reason for this long neglect of your religious duties."

"I never speak of these things to any one but my Confessor," replied Jane with some bitterness.

"Neither would I ask you to do so, if I were satisfied that you had a Confessor. Pray, have you one ?"

" The Church only insists on confession once a year."

"Have you been to confession within the year ?"

The cloud darkened on the girl's brow: "Papa," she said, "it is not right to play the inquisitor. This is an affair which I prefer to keep to myself. It is quite out of your province."

" My child, if you choose to take this tone with me, you will find that I can be severe with you. I desire that you will go to your room immediately, and remain there for the rest of the evening."

There was something in Sir Thomas's voice and eye which his daughter dared not resist. But she swept out of the room with her stateliest air.

" He treats me as if I were a child," she said to herself, when she reached her chamber; "but I won't stand it. A pretty pass things are coming to. O Henry, what have you brought me to ?

If I dared tell the whole truth to Father Cuthbert."

The next morning there was a constraint in every one's manner towards Jane. She tried to brave it out, and before breakfast was over, she turned to Mrs. Blunt, and remarked in an indifferent tone:

"We drive to Lady Clare's, after luncheon, do we not?"

But her father interposed—"Your aunt and sister will go to the garden party; but you will remain at home to-day."

This was a terrible mortification to the pleasure-loving Jane. She caught her sister's eye, which was full of tears. Charlotte dashed them away, and looked appealingly towards their father: but she knew better than to venture on a word of remonstrance.

Jane had a long dull afternoon, roaming about the garden and the shrubbery, and concocting her plans.

"This will never do"—she thought, "I must throw our tyrant off the scent. He is so truthful himself, that I shall be able to blindfold him. I know what I will do."

When the ladies returned from their party, Charlotte sought her sister, and throwing an arm round her neck, said imploringly—"Jane, darling, you make me unhappy as well as yourself. Go to papa, there's a dear, and make it up with him."

Now the best and the softest point in Jane's character, was a certain fondness for her eldest sister; though there was an alloy of jealousy in it. On this occasion, however, she was obstinate, and replied—

"I shall do no such thing, Charlotte. But don't think me unkind: if you only knew how miserable I am !"

"But why should you be, dearest? we have so much to make us happy."

"You have such a bright disposition; and you are always doing good."

Charlotte looked anxiously at her sister, and said: "If you have any sorrow that we do not know of, it might relieve your mind to tell it to us."

"There may be reasons why I cannot do this," said Jane; "there are burdens which one must bear alone. There! I have broken my resolution in telling you so much. For Heaven's sake, don't let papa think that I have anything on my mind."

"But why not make a friend of him? There is no one I know, who can comfort as he can: and he would be pleased with your confidence," she added in her most caressing manner.

"Impossible!" exclaimed Jane, "and mind I shall never tell you a word, unless you promise to keep my counsel."

"Never fear," said Charlotte: hereupon the dinner-bell rang, and the sisters went to the drawing-room.

There were no further signs of contest between Sir Thomas and his daughter. Having made her feel the weight of his displeasure, he said no more. One Saturday, about a fortnight afterwards, the carriage was ordered to take Miss Maxwell to St. Margaret's, the church which she usually frequented for Confession. Jane thought proper to join her sister, and to Charlotte's great relief, took her place among Father Cuthbert's penitents. But it was not for Penance that she presented herself at the sacred tribunal. Her heart was in that surging state, so full of passion and misery, that a vent of some sort had become essential to her.

"Father, I have not come to you for any good," she began, "but because I cannot help it. If parents are tyrants, it makes children hypocrites. Papa won't be satisfied unless I make a pretence of coming to the Sacraments. But I am going to tell you something, which will prove whether I am a fit person for Absolution."

"Calm yourself, my child," said Father Cuthbert, "this is not the first time that I have listened to a tale of sorrow."

"Father, you know that I went to Switzerland last year with Aunt Edith. We were at Lucerne for two months. I used to go to Mass in the morning. There was an English family, who had a country house in the neighbourhood, with whom we were very intimate. There was

a son, who paid me great attentions. Aunt
Edith was a regular dragon, and kept me out of
his way, as much as she could. But he used to
manage to join me on my way to church. At
first I tried to get rid of him; but it was of no
use. He seemed to worship the ground I trod
upon."

"Why did you not tell your aunt?"

"Because she always set herself against him.
Well, Father, the end of it was, I got to like
him!"

"To like him very much," said the Priest;
"it is as I thought; go on, dear child."

"The day before we left Lucerne, he per-
suaded me to take a quiet walk with him; we
came to a wood which contains a shrine of our
Lady. We sat down in the shade: and he con-
fided to me, how much he loved me. But he
told me at the same time that his religion was
different from mine, and that he had never been
baptized. He wanted me to engage myself to
him, but said that it must be a secret for the present, until the death of a certain aunt, from

whom he expected money, and who would never forgive him if he married a Catholic.   He seemed half wild with grief at the thought of our approaching separation.   He took my hand in his, and declared that he would never let it go until I plighted my troth to him.   Just then the bell of the chapel began to ring the Angelus. I knew it was a warning from Heaven: but, Father, I could not resist him—he is so clever and attractive—I knew it was a sin—but—"

"You gave him the promise which he asked. It grieves me, child, to think that after the excellent education which you have received, you should have so far forgotten yourself as to walk alone with this person.   But let me tell you, that your supposed engagement with him is null and void.   The Church permits no Sacramental union between her children and the unbaptized."

" But he holds our engagement as valid," said the girl ; " and I don't intend to give him up."

" And for this man, who could so tamper with your youth and inexperience, you have withdrawn all this time from the Sacraments of the Church ?"

"Yes, Father; I don't pretend to excuse myself. But O, I cannot give up this sweet sin !"

" It is doubly a sin in you, because God called you to something better. I have never changed my opinion as to your vocation to the religious life. If Almighty God ever called any one to the cloister, He called you; and, what is more, you know it."

"Yes; I was very happy for the first half-year. But I could not help having a nasty novice mistress, who spoiled my vocation."

" It was your own wicked temper which spoiled your vocation. And, mark me, you will have no peace of mind until you do what you know that God requires of you."

" Almighty God cannot be such a tyrant as to ask people to commit moral suicide. I could no more give up Henry than I could give up my own soul."

"What did you mean, when you told me the

other day that you had lost your belief in every thing good ?"

"Because when papa found out that I had something which I did not like to tell him, he became utterly unjust: he watched my correspondence, stopped my letters, frightened me by his lectures, and drove me frantic by his suspicions. But he thinks it is all over now. Good people are odious !"

"I don't know a better man than your father," said the Priest. "If your conduct had been everything that a young lady's ought to be, he would have had no cause for suspicion."

"I shall hate you, Father, if you take his part."

"Honour thy father and thy mother," said the Priest, impressively.

"And now, Father, give me your blessing, and I will go away."

"No, my child; to-day I shall punish you by withholding my blessing, in order to bring you to a sense of the sinfulness of your present conduct."

"It is of no consequence," said the girl, as she rose to depart, but she felt deeply pained and humiliated, as Father Cuthbert well knew, for she had venerated him from her earliest years. There was a holy power in him which had always impressed her. From her childhood he had treated her with a mixture of kindness and firmness, and he had more influence over her than any one in the world.

CHAPTER III.

"Ever their phantoms rise before us,
  Our nobler brothers, though one in blood :
At bed and table they lord it o'er us,
  With looks of beauty, and words of good."

STERLING.

SIR THOMAS MAXWELL had a youthful ward who had been brought up at the same convent school with his daughter Agnes, and the two girls returned home together. In order to describe Agnes duly, the artist would have to dip his pencil in the colours of light. If ever there was a beau ideal in the present century of what the Virgin martyr must have been when on earth, it was the youngest Miss Maxwell at the age of

eighteen. She was tall, fair, and graceful—
bright as the summer morning. Her blue eye
was the reflection of a beautiful soul, and she
generally wore her hair, which was of shadowy
gold, twined in rich plaits round her classical
head. She and Miss Raymond were inse-
parable.

Leila, for that was the Christian name of
Sir Thomas's ward, was a girl on whom no one
could look without being interested. She was
small, and had the figure of a sylph—so ex-
quisitely fashioned, that you could not help
watching every movement she made — she
seemed the impersonation of elegance. She
wore her raven hair in a profusion of curls; she
had the rich colouring of the children of the
south, and her dark eye gave evidence of a soul
of fire. She was affluent and generous, and
adored Agnes. She would have spent half her
income in making presents to her pet, only that
young lady was too independent to accept gifts
which she could not reciprocate. But there
was one person to whom Leila was even more

devoted, and that was her guardian. The no-
bility of his character had seized on her ardent
imagination; his kindness had won her heart,
and the power of his intellect had captivated hers.

About a month after her return home, Sir
Thomas was sitting in his library, which, though
it contained great literary treasures, was fur-
nished with extreme plainness and simplicity.
There was a considerable dash of asceticism in
the Baronet's character. He strictly observed
the fasts of the Church, and added many others
out of his private devotion. There was a tap
at the door, and when Sir Thomas said, "Come
in," behold, it was Leila.

"Welcome, dear child," he said, and a smile
of rare beauty, for it seemed to come from a
region holier than this world of ours, illuminated
his countenance.

"Do I interrupt you, father?" for so she
always called him.

"Never, little lady; I am always at your ser-
vice. Show me how I can promote your happiness this morning."

There was one footstool in the room. Leila drew it close to her guardian, and perched herself airily upon it.

"I want to be good," she began, "and I don't know how. I want to be very happy, too."

"I think you want something to do, Leila. Your time hangs on hand. Charlotte comes and reads with me for an hour every morning. I think you had better come with her."

Leila gave a quick look of delight, and Sir Thomas continued:

"I am a great advocate for intellectual cultivation. I don't approve of idle or frivolous ladies; then why should not you go with her when she visits the schools and the poor, and learn to make yourself useful?"

"Yes, but Charlotte is so awfully good—I should find it fatiguing to be always good."

"No one wishes to prevent you from having your fair share of recreation and amusement, my child. But life is a serious thing, and we shall have to give an account both of our time and our talents. With your good fortune, and the good education which you have had, you may do a great deal for God's glory."

"Very well, I will begin. I have plenty of ambition. I hope that is not a fault."

"Not if it is well directed."

Leila got up and walked to the open window, whence she beheld Agnes strolling in the flower-garden; so she ran back to Sir Thomas, kissed his hand in a half childish way, and left him to join her friend.

"That child has a character," soliloquized her guardian, "which will be potent for good or for evil. She has intelligence and activity, but she is perilously impulsive. I must watch over her, and keep her energies well employed."

That evening there was a suburban meeting for an object of great importance to Catholics. The Bishop was in the chair; and Sir Thomas Maxwell was the most impressive of the speakers on the platform. His oration was long, and was listened to with the greatest attention. Of course, his family was among

the audience. Charlotte and Leila were en-
tranced by his eloquence. He threw his whole
soul into the speech. He spoke with anima-
tion and dignity. Every attitude might have
been a study for sculpture, every inflection of
the voice was full of music. The cheers, when
he finished speaking, were overwhelming. He
was in the habit of making many converts to
our holy religion, by the sheer force of his devoted character. He was a man who thoroughly
enjoyed society, literature, and art. In the
constant performance of duty, he never lost his
hold on the supernatural world. His soul
walked very near to God.

There was some confusion as the assembly
broke up. The four young ladies from the
Elms—that was the name of Sir Thomas's residence—were waiting for their escort, when a
strikingly handsome man made his way towards
Jane, who was a little apart from the others,
and exchanged a few words with her in a low
voice. As he bowed over her hand at parting,
her sisters caught the words, "at Lucerne." He

then made a formal inclination to Charlotte, and went away.

"Who is that gentleman?" said Agnes and Leila in a breath.

"Only an acquaintance whom we met on the Continent," replied Jane; and then she whispered to her eldest sister, "Don't tell papa."

At this moment Sir Thomas joined them, and Jane had no opportunity of speaking again to her sister, till they went to their rooms for the night.   Then she waited for the maid to withdraw, and entered Charlotte's chamber.   She knelt down coaxingly by the bedside, and said, "Darling, you will grant my request—you will make me so happy if you will."

"I don't like these concealments," said Charlotte.   "Papa has a natural right to our confidence.   I think that you ought to tell him yourself."

"Impossible—it would be the ruin of all my hopes."

"Jane," said her sister, with some severity, "you cannot wish to encourage clandestine intercourse with this gentleman : it would be unworthy of you !"

" Of course it would. I solemnly assure you that I have neither seen him nor spoken to him since Christmas, when papa surprised us in the shrubbery, and almost insulted him."

" And when do you expect to see him again ?" enquired Charlotte.

" O I don't know—not for months."

" Didn't he say something about meeting you at Lucerne ? I would not have asked papa to take us there this summer, if I had thought you had any scheme of this kind."

" I want to see his mother, dear ; you know she and I were great friends. It is very doubtful whether he will get leave of absence to run down. There, as I have told you so much, you must promise to keep my counsel. I have been so unhappy," she added, " and now there seems to be a little brightness in store for me. You never would have the heart to throw me back into my misery." And here she burst into tears.

"Don't cry, darling," said Charlotte affectionately, drying her eyes and kissing her. "You know I can't bear telling tales." Her tone wavered for a moment, but she added steadily, "You must promise me that you will not see him again without papa's permission."

"Yes, dear, I promise," said Jane, feeling that the victory was hers.

Leila lay awake all that night, lost in thought. Her one idea was the hero of that evening. He had become, unconsciously to herself, a portion of her very life and being. For two years this wild idolatry had been growing into her soul. During the long intervals of her school life, it had been the romance of which she had thought by day and dreamed by night. She used to rave about him to the nuns; but as she always called him her father, they laughed at her raptures, or gently tried to repress them. His letters to her used to be her principal consolation, and they were full of admirable advice. Since her return home— for such the Elms had been to her for many a long year—the spell had grown more potent. Such was her infatuation, that the air through which he passed in walking was to her full of consecration. He was "the ocean to the river of her thoughts."

"Oh, if he would love me as I love him," she said to herself; "he is fond of me, but he treats me as a child, as his youngest daughter. This ought to be happiness enough for me But I shall have to return to India in the autumn. Oh, if mamma would but leave me here another year. She was very nice, but it is so long since I have seen her—she is more like an idea to me—and he is a reality. Happy are his children, but they don't half know it. Charlotte does; I almost envy her the right she has to worship him. Jane doesn't care for him. There are times when I think she almost hates him. She shrinks from him, as the wicked spirit shrank from the spear of Ithuriel. Agnes, though she loves him, is a little afraid of him. With Charlotte, perfect love seems to cast out fear. Oh, it will kill me to leave him!"

3

The next day Charlotte—whose health was always delicate—had to keep her room from the fatigue and excitement of the previous evening. At eleven o'clock Leila betook herself to the library for the usual hour of study with her guardian.

"You are pale, my child," he said; "late hours do not agree with you. I shall send you to play among the flowers with Agnes this morning."

"Oh, no," she said; "let me stay here—I will not disturb you. You can go on writing if you like;" and so she took a Latin book, and placing herself on the footstool with a certain wilful grace, she pretended to study.

"You are holding that book upside down," remarked Sir Thomas, turning from his desk and bending over. A vivid blush suffused her countenance, and she tossed the book impetuously to the other end of the room.

Sir Thomas regarded her attentively, and said, "You look feverish, child; let me feel your pulse."

She rose from her seat and looked on the ground, but without making any sign of obedience to this request. He took her hand and examined the wrist, which presented no alarming symptoms.

"Now go and pick up my Virgil," he said in a tone which was somewhat severe. She hesitated a moment. "Leila, do as I bid you," he reiterated. All the pride of young ladyhood was rising within her; she did not like to be commanded, even by him. He had generally spoiled her a little in the past, for there was a depth of tenderness in Sir Thomas's nature, and she had always been a special favourite of his. She looked up at him now with those large dark eyes of hers somewhat wistfully, but reading no sign of relenting on the marble brow, or on the firm lips, she burst into tears.

Sir Thomas could never bear to see women cry, and he was greatly annoyed.

"Leila," he exclaimed, "you are too old for these scenes of childish temper. Go to your room, until you can learn to command yourself like a lady."

She was in the act of running away, when he called her back—

" I never allow myself to be disobeyed," said he ; " bring me back my Virgil first."

She picked up the book, and threw it on the table as if it stung her.   Then, with a resentful look at her guardian, she took her departure and slammed the door.

CHAPTER IV.

"The light of love, the purity of grace,
  The mind, the music breathing from her face,
  The heart, whose softness harmonized the whole—
  And Oh ! that eye was in itself a soul."

                             BYRON.

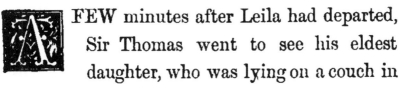FEW minutes after Leila had departed, Sir Thomas went to see his eldest daughter, who was lying on a couch in her room. Agnes, who had been hovering over her sister, saw from an expression in her father's face, that he wished to be alone with the invalid; so she slipped quietly away. It was a pretty room, and tastefully appointed. There was an elegance about everything which Charlotte did, or superintended. You might have seen a great deal of her character in the collec-

tion of choice volumes which her library contained. A few pious images and engravings of rare beauty adorned the room. Agnes, who was the Flora of the family, had just placed a vase of flowers on the table, by the open window. Charlotte had inherited more of her father's mind and soul than either of the other children. There had always been so much intellectual sympathy between them, that from the age of thirteen Sir Thomas had treated her more like a younger sister than a daughter: for his nature was expansive, and Mrs. Blunt was reserved, and not much of a companion to him.

After putting some kind inquiries about her health, Sir Thomas approached the subject which was then making him uneasy, and related what had taken place that morning. Charlotte listened attentively: with a woman's instinct she had already fathomed Leila's secret, and possessed the clue to her strange behaviour.

"Papa darling," she said, "you must remember that Leila is no longer a child."

"Her temper seems more ungovernable than when she was a child."

"I did not mean that exactly; but I think a thorough change would be good for her—to go among fresh people, I mean. I think she is getting morbid and unreal."

"I wish you would have her a great deal with you. She looks up to you, and you might influence her for good. Agnes has a great deal of character, but she is too near her own age."

"Certainly I will, dear papa"—but she added, with an arch expression, which lit up the lilies of her complexion—"you must leave her quite to my management. I think she wants a governess just now, more than a tutor."

Sir Thomas looked puzzled for a moment— "Do you mean that my way of managing her is not the right one?" he asked; for he saw that more was implied than met his ear.

"I think that you are very good and very wise"—said Charlotte, "but there are problems which baffle the cleverest of men."

"But not the cleverest of women!" mischievously suggested her father.

"Certainly not—for the very reason that we are women," responded Charlotte.

Sir Thomas had a great respect for his daughter's understanding, but he had no idea of giving up his influence over his ward. He was greatly attached to her in a paternal fashion. Her pretty little ways amused him. It came naturally to him to rule other minds; and he had great confidence in his own power of doing this well.

The day passed without any overtures from Miss Raymond; but after night prayers, which were said in the library, Leila lingered behind the others, and as soon as the door was shut, she approached her guardian, took his hand betweeen both of hers, and said,

"Father dear, I am very sorry for having been so rebellious this morning—forgive me"—and a little tear fell on the hand which she was clasping.

"I forgive you, my child," he said kindly, "but you must also ask pardon of God, for the pride and anger of which you have been guilty."

"O yes, I will," she said; "I have been so miserable all day; but I could not conquer myself until now."

"You deserved to be miserable, Leila, and you

never will be happy, till you learn to control your predominant passion."

"I am quite happy now," she said: and, indeed, she looked radiant, like the sun after a shower.

" Goodnight, dear child," he said, " don't forget your act of contrition."

" And you are not a bit displeased with me, now ?" she added, looking wistfully up at him.

He stooped and imprinted a fatherly kiss on the girl's forehead, as he had been accustomed to do in her childhood, though he had left off the practice of late. A burning blush suffused her countenance. At this moment, Jane, who had left a prayer-book behind her, returned to the library, candle in hand, and deliberately surveyed the pair before her.

"What do you want, my dear ?" said her father, facing round.

" I am sorry to have interrupted such a pathetic scene," said his daughter, for she was utterly deficient in delicate feeling. Leila rushed by her, and left the room.

"It is time for you to retire to rest," said Sir Thomas, as his daughter lingered, for there was something in her manner which annoyed him.

"I am going directly," said Jane, "but this is a good opportunity for me to say a word, which I have wanted to say for a long time past. Don't be offended at my plain speaking, papa; but, I assure you, that the less petting Leila Raymond gets from you the better. You don't see what all the world sees—that girl is in love with you."

"Do I hear aright?" said Sir Thomas; and there was a severity in his tone before which even Jane, with all her audacity, trembled: "You make me more angry at this moment, than you ever did in your life."

"I dare say I do—but it is time that somebody spoke to you. Charlotte sees it as plainly as I do, only she has not the pluck to tell you the truth, as I have done. She is too high-flown and refined."

At this moment Sir Thomas remembered certain remarks which his eldest daughter had made that morning, and a painful surmise came over his mind. Though he was a man of great natural penetration, he was sometimes in the habit of reading character according to certain preconceptions of his own. On this occasion he was somewhat obstinate, and would not see the light which his daughter held so unceremoniously before his eyes.

"Jane," he exclaimed, "you must be either mad or wicked to think of such a thing!" and his grey eyes flashed under the long black lashes.

"And is Charlotte either mad or wicked?" inquired Jane, with provoking sarcasm.

"Either Charlotte or yourself will incur my severe displeasure if you ever hint at such a possibility as that which you have now suggested. You ought to regard Leila with the tenderness due to a younger sister, and I shall not permit the insane supposition which your impertinence has originated, to hinder the ease of my relations with my adopted child."

"Good Heavens!" cried Jane, "isn't she going back to India in the autumn? It is the proper place for her."

"I wish," said her father, "that you would control the violence of your expressions and of your manner, which is most unlady-like. The sooner you leave my presence the better, for your conduct to-night is simply intolerable. And mark me," he added, his temper rising, "if you presume to say one word to that poor child, such as you have said to me, you will leave this house for the salutary seclusion of a convent."

Jane was under age, and knew that her father was capable of fulfilling this threat. The dull life which she would probably lead as a boarder did not commend itself to her imagination.

The moment that Sir Thomas was alone, he threw himself on his knees before his crucifix, and battled with the storm which was convulsing his soul. Such behaviour from an indifferent person would have wounded his feelings; from a daughter it was almost insupportable.

CHAPTER V.

"Are not the mountains, waves and skies, a part
Of me and of my soul, as I of them?
Is not the love of these deep in my heart,
With a pure passion?"

BYRON.

THE month of August found the Maxwell family established at Lucerne,
with the exception of Charlotte, who
had received a pressing invitation to visit her
old friend, Lady Clare, at Clarendon Park.
Jane had no great love for scenery, she liked
the excitement of people; but the two younger
girls were enraptured by the sight of the Alps.
They had taken up their abode in one of the
best hotels, which overlooks the beautiful lake

of the four Cantons. There was an English lady who had known the family in former times, and who had purchased a house in the neighbourhood. Her name was Mrs. Lawrence; she was the mother of a certain Henry who has been alluded to in these pages. She lost no time in calling on Mrs. Blunt and the young ladies, and she invited them to her pretty château. Sir Thomas had taken the precaution to ascertain that the Captain was in England with his regiment, before he would consent to come to Lucerne. He had no objection to Mrs. Lawrence as an acquaintance for the girls. She professed a great affection for them for their mother's sake. She was a charming person, full of vivacity, and she always had an agreeable circle of friends at her house. She spent the greatest part of the year in Switzerland.

The astonishment of Sir Thomas Maxwell may be conceived when, about a fortnight after their arrival at Lucerne, the captain unexpectedly made his appearance at a fête cham-

pêtre, which was given by his mother in honour
of the English family. It was impossible to be
otherwise than polite to a man, meeting him, so
to speak, on his own ground; still, it was an
embarrassing rencontre, even to the high-bred
courtesy of Sir Thomas. Henry Lawrence had
a good deal of assurance; he made himself delightful to the whole company, and was particularly attentive to Miss Raymond. Jane looked
on with jealous eyes, though she knew that it
was only a piece of policy on her lover's part.

She had never seen Leila look so entrancingly
beautiful, nor had she ever heard her converse
so charmingly. The little witch seemed to have
the art of drawing out all that was brilliant in
Henry; in fact, she was acting a part. She
was aware that her guardian was watching her,
and this gave her the necessary stimulus. He
knew that she was clever, but he was himself
astonished at the quickness of her repartees.
She was asked to sing, and she sang—

" Let me love thee, let me bask in the sunshine of thy
    beauty."

Presently Mrs. Lawrence sat down to the piano, and commenced a waltz. The young people paired themselves immediately. Henry claimed the honour from Leila. She danced like a fairy, or, rather, like an enchantress. When the music finished, Sir Thomas prevented a repetition of the enjoyment, for such it was to Henry, by saying to her gravely, "Don't waltz any more to-night, Leila. If you want an excuse, give the true one, and say that I forbid you."

Their eyes met in a long, searching gaze. Sir Thomas had the art of reading the thoughts of others, while he reserved his own like a splendid enigma.

"You are a tyrant," said Leila, withdrawing her gaze, but she looked all the while as if tyranny from him was sweeter to her than kindness from another. "If you make me give up my pleasure," she added, "you ought to give me something in return. Will you take me away from these hot rooms? Let us go through the shrubbery down to the fountain."

"By all means, little lady," he said, offering her his arm, with a majesty and grace which threw the fascinations of younger men into the shade. And she felt very proud of him as she walked away.

Henry availed himself of this opportunity to exchange a few words with his betrothed, to appoint a time when they might converse uninterruptedly.

"Did you ever see such a flirt?" asked Jane, pointing with her fan to Leila, who was descending the steps from a glass door belonging to the principal salon, on her guardian's arm.

"Of course I know better than to praise one young lady to another," said Captain Lawrence. "But when can I see you alone?"

"Come to our hotel about noon," said Jane.

The next morning she took care not to appear at breakfast, alleging a bad headache as an excuse for remaining in her room. Sir Thomas had ordered a carriage, to take the whole party to a picturesque village about ten miles from Lucerne. The day was splendid; there was a transparency in the atmosphere such as we never see in our northern climes.

"It is a pity that Jane cannot come," remarked Mrs. Blunt, when they were on the point of starting; "and she won't let any one stay with her. She says that she is best alone.'"

Jane heard this remark from her open window. Her headache was a ruse. As soon as the carriage had driven off, she rose, arrayed herself in the neatest of morning dresses, and came down to the salon. She had not been long there when a visitor was announced: no other, of course, than Captain Lawrence. Their interview was long and exciting. It was not an unmixed pleasure to Jane, for she thought that there was a diminution of warmth in her lover's attentions, and she was not slow in attributing this change to the impression which the fascinating Leila had made on him the evening before. They agreed that whenever they might chance to meet in company they were to be particularly guarded, until their plans of action should be matured. Henry declared that the health of his aunt was failing fast, and that they would not have long to wait for the completion of their wishes; meantime the utmost caution must be observed.

They managed to carry out this project of enacting mutual coldness in the presence of others so successfully, that Sir Thomas began to think that his daughter was acquiescing in his wishes.

One fine afternoon he engaged a large boat to take his family and the Lawrences an excursion on the lake. Every one was in capital spirits. They went on shore to partake of coffee, which was laid out in an arbour commanding a fine prospect of mountain, wood, and water. The two gentlemen took a walk afterwards together. It was the captain's policy to propitiate Sir Thomas. By degrees they got into a conversation on religious matters.

" I fancy," began Henry, "that if you and I, Sir Thomas, were to compare notes, we should not be found to differ so broadly as you at this moment may suppose. I have the greatest respect for the Roman Catholic religion, and I very often come to your worship."

"But you do not pray with us, you do not recognize the Sacrifice, which is offered on our altars !"

"There is a great deal in your ceremonies which I admire; and in fact where we have no temple of our own, we come to your churches, as the best and only substitute."

"We cannot accept this conduct of yours," said Sir Thomas, "as any indication of true brotherhood.　It is merely the unconscious homage which error pays to truth.　I believe, sir, I am not mistaken, in assuming you to be a Positivist ?"

Captain Lawrence bowed, and continued— "We worship the same God, though under different conditions.　We have no objection to the representation of the Madonna and Child."

"Pardon me, we do not worship the same God.　The object of our adoration is one God in Three Persons.　You think proper to deify humanity, just as the heathens deified nature.　Your system is analagous, though not identical, with Pantheism. It is not long since I entered the house of a relative of mine, who unfortunately holds your opinions. If I had not been forewarned, I might have been misled by the first sight which met me in the hall, a magnificent representation of the Virgin and Child. But I knew that it was only meant to symbolize nature and humanity. You have endeavoured also to imitate the celestial court of angels and saints, but you have only produced in their stead a set of heroes inferior, in my mind, to old Homer's conceptions; for, at any rate, there was something preternatural about them."

"I suppose you will not deny," said Captain Lawrence, "that our moral practice is better than that of many Christians?"

"I have no wish to deny it," said Sir Thomas; "a universal philanthropy is often more amiable in its fruits than an unswerving theology. But your philosophy will never produce anything above the ordinary line. You will never rise to heroic virtue. You will never emulate some of our saints, whom you cannot help admiring ; and who owed the grandeur of character which moves you, to the supernatural principles which you deny."

"I like a religion," said Captain Lawrence, "that is within my comprehension, something that I can grasp, as I grasp this Alpine rose," and he plucked one.

"For which very reason," rejoined Sir Thomas, "it is no religion, but a simple philosophy. There is no religion without mystery. It is no argument against a dogma, to say that it is incomprehensible. The great God Who made us, —Whom our finite mind can conceive but cannot contain,—'the cup of the finite can support, though it cannot receive the globe of the Infinite'*—has exacted from us that we should believe ; He does not require that we should understand.",

"Then you admit that Christianity is contrary to reason ?"

"It is not against reason, but above reason, as

* Monsignor Capel.

heaven is above earth. We shall understand it all some day, when the light of glory is infused into our intellect. But that is a consummation which you do not even aspire to. You are satisfied to look forward to a state of general absorption in humanity. I cannot conceive the attraction which such a notion can present to any thinking glowing mind, conscious of its own identity, and of its Maker's undying image."

"At any rate," said the Captain, "we escape your dreadful doctrine of eternal flames—"

"In which the justice of God shines, an awfully magnificent attribute—beautiful even in its severity—without which God would be no God. It is only in the God of Christians, in the God Who is represented to us by the Catholic Church, that all opposite perfections are blended in a complete harmony. From His justice, you must turn to the prodigality of His love and mercy. From the dark world of condemned spirits, you must turn to the great universe, with its countless systems, and to the vast heavens, in which millions upon millions of the blessed will so far outnumber the lost, that these latter will seem, perhaps, like a few autumn leaves in comparison with the wealth of summer foliage."

At this point of the conversation, they came round to the garden, where the ladies had finished their preparations for returning home.

Mrs. Lawrence had engaged Jane to bring her work, and spend the next morning at the château. Sir Thomas was rather startled at lunch, when he heard that this invitation had been given and accepted, though he had not the faintest idea how far matters had already gone between Henry Lawrence and his daughter. Jane had hoped to return home in time to avoid questioning; but the Captain had walked part of the way with her, and they had lingered on the road. Sir Thomas reproved the young lady for having gone out alone, and strictly forbade her, during the remainder of their stay at Lucerne, to leave the hotel unattended. A letter from Charlotte arrived about this time.

"Clarendon Park,
"Worcestershire, August 30.

"MY DEAREST PAPA,

"I hope you are all enjoying yourselves as much as I am. We have had a succession of cloudless days. Lady Clare is like a mother in her kindness to me. The house is full of agreeable people. Sir Julius is greatly improved since he made the tour of Europe. But the person who interests me most, is the new chaplain, Father Austin. He belongs to the Third Order of St. Dominick. He is one of the cleverest men whom I ever came across; and he has a way of making religion attractive to every one. He is taking great pains with me just now. Willie is his pupil, and as he is studying for the Church, he gets a theological lecture every morning. Sometimes I coax Lady Clare to bring her knitting and come with me into the study, when this is going on. Father Austin was kind enough to say that we might do so. He is of opinion that it would be a good thing for ladies to get more 'strong teaching,' as he calls it, on the

subject of religion, than is usually thought
necessary.   I never realized the full beauty and
grandeur of many of our doctrines, until I heard
them expounded by him.   And then he has a
way of attracting the heart to God through the
intellect.   He is the strictest Confessor I ever
met, though so kind.   He expects a great deal
more from me in the way of piety, than I have
been in the habit of practising.   It is only to
you, my own very dear papa, that I should men-
tion these things; but writing to you is like
communing with one's own soul.

" Your most affectionate

" CHARLOTTE."

And indeed it was true that Father Austin
was doing God's work for Miss Maxwell; and
he was doing it in no ordinary way.   He found
in her a disciple, whose elevated mind and generous soul could appreciate his high teaching.
He pointed out to her her faults with a father's
frankness.   Her nature was sensitive and fas-
tidious to a degree : in fact, she was a little over

refined:—he taught her to place a value on mortification. She was naturally proud and fond of ruling others, with that pretty graceful sceptre of hers—he taught her how to obey. Though she had acquired considerable mastery over a quick temper, there was still a great deal of impetuosity connected with her ardent feelings and strong affections, which stood in need of a curb. This visit to Clarendon Park was an era in her life, and in the history of her mind. From this time she resolved to devote herself to the practice of perfection, as far as it is attainable in the world. It was the first time that she had met with an ecclesiastic who thoroughly comprehended her, and who had both the ability and the leisure to cultivate the holy aspirations and tendencies which were the product of Divine grace. She resolved to make him her director for the future, and to be altogether obedient to his counsels.

CHAPTER VI.

"There are fatal days indeed,
In which the fibrous years have taken root,
So deeply, that they quiver to their tops,
Whene'er you stir the dust of such a day."

BROWNING.

AGNES and Leila occupied the same apartment. Their wondows commanded a magnificent view of the Alps. They were sitting together on the same couch one evening, admiring the beauty of the scene.

"Life is worth having, if it were only to enjoy such a view as this," said Agnes.

"Yes, darling," said Leila rather absently, "I used to be mad about scenery, but of late I think that I have got to live more upon ideas.

Can you guess," she added, with a sudden change of manner, "what makes Jane so cross and spiteful to me ?"

" I think I can," said Agnes, while a sensitive blush deepened the rose on her cheek.

"I wish you would tell me then," urged Leila, drawing closer to her friend.

"It is evident," said Agnes, "that Captain Lawrence admires you."

"Well, what of that?" said Leila, shaking her dark curls.

"It is also evident that Jane likes Captain Lawrence. "

"Yes," said Leila, "she always acts as if she had a right to monopolize him, but abstains from doing it. I have never seen him pay her any marked attentions."

"I suspect," said Agnes, "from something Charlotte told me, that there was more between them last year than we were aware of. Don't you remember she tried to make a mystery of their acquaintance, on the night of the meeting, before we left home ?"

"She needn't be jealous of me," remarked Leila; "I don't care two straws for him."

"Then I wouldn't make myself quite so agreeable to him," responded Agnes.

"Oh," said Leila, with a conscious blush, for the little puss knew that she had done her best to be fascinating, not with the view of enchaining Captain Lawrence, but in the idle hope of piquing her guardian, who had reproved her once or twice for this conduct; then she hid her face in Agnes's drapery.

"You know that you have been very naughty, Leila," continued Agnes, with a pretty attempt at scolding. "I wonder that you like to displease papa, by doing what he so manifestly disapproves."

"Hush, here he comes," said Leila, her quick ear detecting the beloved footstep as he approached the door.

"Can I come in?" he asked. "I want you two young ladies to take a walk with me this evening. We shall be just in time to catch the sunset from the Gutch. Jane is occupied with her aunt in the salon."

"Oh, how delightful!" cried both the girls in a breath.

In a few minutes they were equipped, and ascending the mountain side with Sir Thomas. When they came to a convenient spot they sat down on the grass, and gazed upon a firmanent of glory. The snowy Alps caught and reflected the rays of the departing sun, and the sky was all gold and vermilion.

"Fair image of a fairer world!" said Sir Thomas; then, after a pause, he added, " I have something to tell you, children, which Charlotte already knows by letter. I hope there is a happy future in store for all of you. As soon as I have made certain arrangements for the advantage of my daughters—my four daughters"— and he gave an expressive glance towards Leila —"I shall be free to follow the vocation which our good God has given me."

"Papa!" cried Agnes, breathless with surprise.

Leila did not speak, but her cheek turned as pale as the white piqué dress she wore.

"Do you guess what I mean?" said Sir

Thomas. "I have an ambition to enter the Priesthood, and end my days at the altar."

Agnes was deeply moved; she lifted his hand to his lips, and murmured, "My own dear papa!"

"What's the matter?" exclaimed the baronet abruptly, for the lady on the other side of him was lying on the grass insensible.

"She has fainted!" cried Agnes, more terrified than surprised. The truth broke on Sir Thomas. Some water was procured from the nearest brook; but it was a long time before Leila was sufficiently recovered to return home. From that hour Sir Thomas avoided being alone with his ward. His heart was full of a deep compassion for her; there was a kind thoughtfulness in his eye whenever it rested upon her, but he seldom spoke to her. He felt that they must part, but he wished to do nothing abruptly.

A few days after they were to spend an evening at the château. Agnes regarded Leila anxiously, as she was completing her toilet.

The latter had scarcely slept for some nights past, and her cheeks had grown pale. Agnes had carefully avoided making the slightest allusion to the scene on the Gutch. Just now there was a strange light in Miss Raymond's eye, and a sort of desperate resolution in her manner. She wore a dress of black silk, flounced to the waist, which swept the ground. She put on her jet ornaments, and adjusted one white rose in her raven hair, and another in the bosom of her dress.

Mrs. Lawrence had invited a large party. Miss Raymond made herself agreeable to every one, and especially to the Captain. There was a fascination about her which positively bewildered him. He was ceasing to care for Jane, though he intended to keep his word and marry her. In the meantime why should he not enjoy the society of this brilliant girl, whom it was his duty to entertain?

During an interval, after refreshments had been partaken of, while preparations were being made for dancing, Jane gave a somewhat impe-

5

rious signal to her betrothed that he was to follow her into the flower-garden. As soon as they got into a shady avenue she could keep her temper no longer, and commenced an attack on him for his open flirtation with Miss Raymond.

"I thought it was your own wish," he replied, "that we were to enact that little double game, to draw off attention from ourselves."

"Yes, but you are going too far; that girl, who is a *diablesse,* is positively fooling you. And yet she doesn't care for you a bit: I know that for a fact."

"You seem to be very certain about the state of another young lady's heart," he said rather mockingly.

"Why you must be an idiot," she retorted, "if you don't see that one hair of my father's head is dearer to her than all the rest of the world. The little fool won't get him though!"

Jane had her reasons for not confiding her parent's intentions of becoming a Priest to her betrothed.

"Miss Raymond is a mere child compared to Sir Thomas Maxwell," remarked the Captain.

"She is, without exception, the deepest girl I ever came across. I can't think what you can see in her to admire, unless it be her fortune. But you men are all alike," she added with a sneer; "a pretty face is very well, but money is still better."

"You don't mean to insinuate that you are sketching my character at the present moment?"

"Indeed I do; I think you are capable of anything, after the fickleness that I have seen in you."

"Miss Maxwell," he said, "I must insist on your at once withdrawing the insinuation which you have just made against my honour as a gentleman."

"You only want a pretext to break off our engagement," she exclaimed.

"You had better say that again!" said he.

"I say it again," she cried, half beside herself with jealousy and mortification.

"Then all is over between us. Ladies are privileged to say a great deal, but they have no right to take away a man's character to his face."

"It is as I thought," she said. "You have been only waiting for an excuse to break off. But you won't get your golden idol! Papa will take good care of that. You are a false, deceitful man."

"I am thankful that you have shown yourself in your true colours before it was too late. But I would have kept my troth to you if you had behaved yourself. Miss Maxwell, I have the honour of bidding you adieu—I see your sister coming."

He made an obeisance to each of the young ladies, and departed. Jane could almost have bitten off her tongue, in her rage and self-vexation for the fatal words which she had uttered. She could not make her appearance again in company, nor could she bring herself to explain to Agnes what had happened. She got a servant to order the carriage, and requested her sister to make an excuse of sudden indisposition to their father and hostess. Agnes wished to return to the hotel with her, but Jane would not hear of this. Agnes was too truthful to utter any prevarication; she merely announced that her sister felt unequal to rejoin the party.

Captain Lawrence had the felicity of a round dance with Leila. Sir Thomas looked on for a moment in amazement, for he had forbidden his ward to waltz with any one a few days previously. He then walked out into the grounds to avoid a sight so painful to him as the open and flat disobedience of a girl whom he had loved and cherished as a daughter. When there was a pause in the music, Captain Lawrence whispered a few words of admiration in Miss Raymond's ear. She said nothing, but looked up with one of her glorious smiles. Soon after this, Sir Thomas gave the signal for the return home.

"Give me the rose from your corsage," said the Captain, as he placed Leila in the carriage, by the side of Agnes. The request had just been complied with, as Sir Thomas turned from bidding adieu to his hostess.

The next morning, Jane was really ill, and her aunt was in attendance on her. After breakfast, Sir Thomas desired Agnes to go and see her sister. He then drew a chair to the verandah, where Leila was sitting, and apparently reading a novel, and commenced—

" Though you seem to have lost all regard for my wishes, child— you must remember that you are still under my authority, until your mother has you again under her protection. I did not choose to make a scene last night, by interfering, as I had the right to do, between yourself and Captain Lawrence. But I insist upon it, that you cease to encourage his attentions to yourself. I was shocked to see the way in which you flirted with him yesterday."

" He admires me, and he cares for me," said Leila, fixing her dark eyes on her guardian.

" He is a man, who, though the son of an old friend, was not allowed by me to pay his addresses to one of my daughters. In that light I have always regarded you. Will you give me your word of honour, that you will encourage him no more ?"

" I don't know what you mean," said Leila evasively; "one can't help being civil to people."

" Have any letters passed between you ?"

" No," faltered the girl, with her eyes on the ground. Now it happened that very morning, that a bouquet had found its way to Miss Raymond's dressing-table, and there was a note twined among the flowers.

" Do you decline giving me the promise I require ?" asked Sir Thomas.

Leila was in a defiant humour, and for the moment she seemed to forget whom she was dealing with : she replied with the air of a princess, " I do."

Her guardian rose, and left the room. About an hour afterwards, he returned, and informed his ward that every arrangement was made for her immediate return to England, in company with Mrs. Blunt. They were to start that evenin . Jane, not being in a condition to travel would remain at Lucerne with himself and Agnes. Leila was thrown into a state of despair by this announcement. There was something in Sir Thomas's manner which betokened an unswerving resolve. She went up to him, she took his hand, she tried some of her coaxing ways.

"My own father," she said, "forgive me this time, and I will promise any thing you like."

And she looked up at him imploringly—at that moment she was bewilderingly pretty. There was a world of softness and supplication in those dark eyes. Sir Thomas was not a man insen- sible to personal charms. Quite the contrary : his artistic eye appreciated beauty under all cir- cumstances ; but he had a rare and marvellous dominion over the realm of sense. He looked down upon her, and said quite calmly—

"I forgive you, child, but you must take the punishment of your disobedience."

"O do not send me away," she pleaded; "the time will be so short before the autumn comes, and I shall have to leave you all. O, for Agnes' sake, spare me—do not separate us yet. It will break my heart," and she burst into tears.

Sir Thomas looked at her with pity—she had been very dear to him in the past. He was in the act of so far relaxing his decision as to think of sending Agnes home with her—when his eagle eye, which nothing escaped, caught sight of a letter on the ground, which Leila had unconsciously drawn out, along with her handkerchief. The handwriting was Captain Lawrence's. He picked it up, and showed it to her.

"Treacherous girl!" he exclaimed in real anger, "you have deceived me!"

"O give me my letter," she cried—"you could not read a letter addressed to another person."

"I have a perfect right to read this one," said Sir Thomas; "but instead of doing so, I shall send it back to the writer. And you have descended to this baseness," he added, "for the sake of a man, for whom you do not care a straw!"

"You are cruel," she exclaimed; "cruel and tyrannical."

"I restrain you with a firm hand," he said,

"that you may not rush to your own destruction."

"Captain Lawrence would not injure me—he is a man of honour."

"But he does not even profess himself a Christian. Leila, though you have lost my respect, and forfeited my affection, I will save you from this precipice!"

"You had better be careful what you do," she said; "I should be a desperate person, if I were driven to extremities!"

"I am quite aware of that," he said with his look of power, before which the excited girl trembled. And yet she had never loved him so much as she did at that moment, she had never admired him so much—her manner suddenly changed—she fell on her knees, she kissed his hand, and cried—

"O do what you like with that letter! do what you like with me! only do not send me away—let me be your child again!"

Sir Thomas was deeply moved—if she had not deceived him, he might have changed his

purpose, but he could not trust her. He felt
with the instinct of a noble-minded man, that
her love for him, even with all its wildness, was
pure as the untrodden snow which lay on the
mountain heights before them. But he knew
that it must be repressed in time, and that
separation was inevitable, at least for a while,
until the electricity should have departed from
her affection, like lightning from a summer
cloud. As for himself, such was the calibre of
his mind, and such the loftiness of his high resolve—that he could pass among the young and
the fair as safely and securely as the Archangel
Gabriel might have done. There was a holy
grandeur on his marble brow, and there was a
vibration of irresistible pathos in his voice, as
he raised the girl from her humble position, and
said—

"You must not remain at my feet, Leila,
though the temporary humiliation was good for
you. It is better that we should part: though
you do not know what it costs me to send you
away!"

She caught her advantage—she seized his hand, and covered it with repentant tears—

"O I am so sorry," she exclaimed; "I would give my life not to have displeased you. I have been very much in the wrong, but forgive me, dearest father, as you hope to be forgiven!"

It was almost more than he could bear—the presence of so much beauty and affection dissolved in tears. But he thought of her soul—already he began to feel like a priest, so he replied in a tone which went straight to her heart—

"I forgive you, child, but I cannot reverse my decision." She clenched his hand in her fairy fingers, but he drew it away, and added—"The only way in which you can regain my good opinion, is by acquiescing in my will at the present crisis. If you are obedient now, and turn over a new leaf for the future, you may get back my regard. Leila, I never thought that you would try me as you have done!"

When the elfish thing saw that her entreaties, and even her endearments, were of no avail, her pride was deeply wounded, and she left him in silence.

She would not trouble herself to make the least preparation for the impending journey; but, at the appointed hour, she found all her luggage arranged in the vestibule, and Mrs. Blunt said to her, quite as a matter of course, "Now, dear, put on your hat, for my brother has ordered the carriage."

Leila felt that resistance would be useless and undignified. Sir Thomas accompanied them to the station, and in a few days they were again domesticated at the Elms.

To describe Miss Raymond's state of mind during the month which followed, would be simply impossible. She was almost delirious with grief. She wandered about the house and grounds like a haunting spirit, and she fancied that she could realize what theologians mean when they talk of "the pain of loss." The presence which had been the joy of her life was withdrawn, and earth had become a horrible blank.

In the meantime, Charlotte had received the letter which informed her of her father's vocation. It was a fearful blow to her—a desolating stroke. She could hardly bring herself to contemplate a life without that beloved companionship. For the first few days after receiving the news, she was so prostrated that Lady Clare was seriously apprehensive about her health.

Father Austin did his best to comfort her. The vicinity of a holy and supernatural person is of itself a great support on these occasions.

"Father," said Charlotte, when they were alone together, " I know it is very wrong of me. I ought to be glad that papa has chosen the better part."

"My dear child," said the Priest, "do not reproach yourself. You are full of enthusiasm. You go on like a rushing river, and a thing like this knocks you down."

" Indeed it does—I feel that I have made an idol of him. He is more than all the world to me, dearer to me than my very soul."

"And therefore, dear child, our Divine Lord, Who wishes to attract you to Himself, takes away your idol, in order that you may love Him more perfectly. He has so few lovers in this world, that those who can—His own special children like yourself—must try to love Him with all their affections. Offer up this heavy cross to Jesus Christ, and throw yourself into His arms, with an act of trusting resignation."

"Yes, Father, I will try, but at present I feel stunned."

"Of course you do, and you need not be discouraged. A sensitive soul is capable of a more intimate union with our dear Lord than a person with less feeling."

"Oh, how good it is of you to say that; but I shall feel crushed all my life, I know I shall."

"Not all your life, my child. Though you are not aware of it, there is an elasticity in your mind and character which will assert itself in due time."

And so it proved. Though Charlotte keenly felt the wound, she was too unselfish to inflict her depression on others, after the first week or two. And the attempt to seem cheerful for the sake of her friends—who could not bear to see her pale cheeks, heavy eyes, and languid manner—assisted her to recover in some degree the balance of her mind. She was glad, however, to make Leila's return to the Elms an excuse for shortening her visit at Clarendon Park. This was a great disappointment to Sir Julius, who had become deeply attached to her, and who even envied Father Austin his province as consoler. He took an opportunity of acknowledging to his mother how very dear Miss Maxwell was to him. Lady Clare would have liked nothing better than such an alliance, but she felt that Charlotte was entrusted to her, and she would not consent to any declaration of affection from Sir Julius until he should have spoken to the young lady's father. For this reason she made less objection than she would have otherwise done to Charlotte's returning home somewhat earlier than was intended.

Sir Thomas had apprised his eldest daughter of all that had taken place at Lucerne. She felt deeply for Leila, and did all she could to comfort her, but in vain. There was a rebellious spirit in the latter which refused consolation. She telegraphed to her mother in India that she was not to expect her, before the spring. Mrs. Raymond was astonished at the independence of this proceeding; but as she was in the act of contemplating second marriage, it rather suited her convenience.

CHAPTER VII.

"And to be wroth with one we love,
Doth work like madness in the brain."
COLERIDGE.

ABOUT the end of October, Sir Thomas Maxwell and his two younger daughters returned to the Elms. Jane had conceived a violent hatred towards Leila, and their meeting was a most painful one. Sir Thomas only remained in England for a fortnight, as he had decided to go to Rome for the next few months, and to take Charlotte with him. This was indeed a delight to her, the best remedy he could have devised to cheer her drooping spirits. He was not misled by the gaiety which she strove to assume: he saw how deeply the arrow had entered into her heart. He found a letter awaiting him from Sir Julius Clare, requesting his paternal permission to propose to Miss Maxwell. Sir Thomas thought that this might be a happy diversion to his daughter's mind, and he called her into the library to show her the letter.

"Sir Julius will have my warmest approval," he remarked; "there is no man I know on whom I would bestow the hand of my darling child so readily."

"No, dear papa," said Charlotte, "do not let him think of me. I have a great esteem for him, but that is all."

"Perhaps it is all that you are expected to have just at present," said Sir Thomas with an arch smile; "'the way to love, thy lord must show!'"

"But I can't bear the thought of it," said Charlotte. "No, dear papa, put it out of your mind; I know you are anxious for my happiness, but it would not make me happy to marry

Sir Julius Clare—or, indeed, any one," she added, with unusual decision.

"It is premature," observed her father, "to make any pledges on the subject; but of course you are free to act as you please. I can only give you my advice, and that I do most strenuously. I counsel you to reconsider the matter. I will give you three days to ponder over it."

"I will do any thing you wish, dearest; but I know what my answer will be."

"Do not let any of your romantic and ultrarefined ideas blind you to the advantages which are offered you by this alliance. It would be a great relief to my mind to see you happily united to one who is in every way worthy of you."

"But supposing," said Charlotte, falling on one knee by her father's side, and tenderly embracing him, "that from a desire for perfection I preferred to think only of our Divine Lord?"

"In that case," replied Sir Thomas, pressing her to his heart, "I have not a word more to say. You are, without exception, the most precious thing which God has ever given me. The King of Heaven has a right to reclaim His own gift! Tell me, my own child, do you wish to enter Religion?"

"I think not, dear papa; but Father Austin has pointed out to me that I may lead a spiritual life in the world—that I may be an Ancilla Domini without entering a cloister."

"Well, dear child, I think you ought to write to your director, and if he approves of your decision at the present crisis, I will convey your rejection to Sir Julius in the kindest terms I can. But would you really like to live on here, after I am gone, under the protection of your aunt, without a definite object in life?"

"I should have a definite object," said Charlotte, with a tremor in her voice, as she thought of the parting that was to come; "there are plenty of poor and sick people in the neighbourhood, besides ignorant persons who want instruction."

"God bless you!" said her father fervently.

Sir Thomas took care to see very little of

Leila during his stay in town. He resolved on this line of conduct for her good, hoping thereby to diminish the poor girl's infatuation. But Miss Raymond's mind was ill regulated, and her will was untamed. She was too proud to intrude on his presence: in fact she tried hard to hate him. On the occasions when they met, his manner to her was gentle, though of course reserved, while hers in return was alternately cold and defiant. Towards Jane he had been particularly tender since the last party at Mrs. Lawrence's. She did not choose to confide in him, or to tell him anything of what had happened; but he saw that she was unhappy, and he tried to cheer her. Her nature was a resentful one; she could not forgive the way in which he had repulsed the Captain at an earlier stage of their acquaintance. Still she could not help being affected by the sympathy of such a parent, all the more that he asked no questions. He knew from Agnes that there had been a scene between Jane and her former lover.

Sir Julius Clare was greatly distressed by Miss Maxwell's rejection of his suit. Lady Clare spent part of the winter in London, and often invited the young ladies of the Elms to her house, after Sir Thomas and Charlotte had set out for the Eternal City. Jane did not choose to wear the willow, so she accepted every invitation that came to her.

One evening, as she was in the act of entering the drawing-room before dinner, she perceived Leila crouched on the hearthrug, reading a letter by the firelight. She advanced stealthily, and before Miss Raymond was aware that she was in the room, she was bending over her, and taking a survey of the handwriting, which she recognized in a moment. She made a dash at the letter.

"How dare you?" exclaimed Leila.

"How dare you receive letters in secret, contrary to the orders of your guardian?" demanded the other.

Jane was in the act of trying to get possession of the epistle, when Mrs. Blunt made her appearance.

"What, quarrelling!" she said; "this must not be, young ladies. I am quite shocked."

Jane turned to her aunt, and cried, "You have reason to be; Miss Raymond is carrying on a clandestine correspondence with a gentleman."

"I am very sorry," said Mrs. Blunt, turning to the accused; "what will your mother say? What will your guardian say?"

But Leila was reckless. "I don't care what they say," she said. "Jane, you are a wicked, cruel girl!"

"I cannot allow this," said Mrs. Blunt. "Let me see your letter, Leila."

"Never," said the girl; "no one has any right to interfere with my correspondence."

"Have you no fear of what Sir Thomas may say or do, when he hears of this?"

"None," said Leila, desperately. "I fear nothing in this world, or in the next. If you will excuse me, I will retire to my room, without encountering the ceremony of dinner to-day."

Miss Raymond was always graceful, even when most excited. She made a courteous bend to Mrs. Blunt, and went to her chamber, locking the door. It was not long before Agnes followed her there, with the wing of a chicken.

"Go away, darling," cried Miss Raymond; "I can't eat, and I want to be alone."

But Agnes would take no refusal, and after a considerable parley, she won admittance.

"My own Leila," she began, "tell me about your trouble. There is nothing I would not do for you."

"But you can do nothing, dearest. Jane is a *diablesse!* I hate the very sight of her!"

"I am sorry that she has been unkind to you. But you see, dear, you had put yourself in the wrong by writing letters in secret. I would not have believed it of you."

"Oh, you are a very pretty lecturer," said Leila; "but when the people whom we most trusted in, turn against us, it makes one feel ready for anything."

"You mean papa; he has not turned against

you. There are few things that he cares for more than he does for your welfare."

"But he has been cruel to me. There is a vein of marble in his character."

"Look back on your life," said Agnes; "has any one ever loved and cherished you more than my father has done?"

"No one," exclaimed Leila; "and the worst of it is, I love him still. To no one but you, who have been more than a sister to me, would I make this confession. I suppose you are shocked at my caring so much for a man, who does not return my affection."

"Leila, dearest," said her friend, "I think that there is great allowance to be made for you. You did not know what you were about, you were so young and inexperienced. But now, for your own peace of mind, for your own dignity as a woman, you must try to turn your thoughts into another channel."

"Perhaps I do," said Leila, "but it is all in vain; his image has become an *idée fixe*, burning into my brain."

"And feeling as you do, you can condescend to trifle with another man ?"

"Who said it was trifling ?" asked Miss Raymond, raising her dark eyes to those of Agnes.

"If it is serious, so much the worse," said her friend; "but I cannot believe it. You would not be so wicked as to give your hand to one man, while your heart was occupied by another. And I am sure you could not resolve so utterly to grieve and disappoint papa."

"Don't be too sure of that. I am glad that it is still in my power to make him feel on my account. I should like to make him feel a little pain, in return for what he has inflicted on me."

"I never knew that you were revengeful before," said Agnes, rising from her chair in beautiful indignation.

"Don't leave me in anger," cried Leila; ". come back and kiss me."

And the little witch looked so forlorn that Agnes was touched.

"Promise me that you will put away these

evil thoughts," she said, as she pressed her lips
to the young girl's brow.

Leila murmured something which was incomprehensible.

Of course Miss Raymond was encompassed
with stricter vigilance than ever after this
occurrence.

Sir Thomas and Charlotte enjoyed their
winter at Rome beyond measure. They found,
as all good and fervent Catholics must find,
that their faith and fervour were alike increased
by coming in contact with the very soul and
centre of Christendom. They assisted at the
Holy Father's Mass on Christmas-day, and
heard the silver trumpets. At Santa Sabina
they met Father Austin, who had come to
Rome for a few weeks on business. He was a
tertiary of the Dominican Order. This rencontre was a great pleasure to all parties. Sir
Thomas invited the Priest to dine at his hotel.
They were kindred spirits, and it was a delight
to Charlotte to listen to their conversation.
Still she was pained to perceive certain symp-

toms of delicate health in Father Austin, which she had not noticed during her stay in Worcestershire. He would not acknowledge that he was ill, and seemed in good spirits. Time fled away on wings of light. Our friends were presented to the Holy Father, who took a great interest in them, and gave his special blessing on Sir Thomas' project of entering the priesthood. In the midst of their happiness, the following letter arrived from Agnes :—

"The Elms, Feb. 10.

"MY DEAREST PAPA,

"I am grieved to tell you that Leila has disappeared, and we do not know where she has gone. Ever since you left home she has been silent and abstracted. Lady Clare did all she could in the way of kindness to win her affection and restore her spirits, but it had not the least effect upon her. Aunt Edith obeyed your directions, and kept the closest watch on every letter that came to the house for her. We think that she must have had an accomplice in her maid, for she managed to hear from that man ⠒ but I am sure she does not care for him. It strikes me that hers is a nature to love once— deeply, perhaps wildly—but never to love again. Latterly she was painfully reserved, even with me. We have made every inquiry about her, but without success. She has arranged her affairs cleverly. Captain Lawrence has not been heard of at his club recently, nor at his usual address. Aunt Edith has written to his mother to inquire where he is, as we cannot help coupling him, in our fears, with Leila's sudden departure."

A week after the receipt of this letter, Sir Thomas and his eldest daughter were again at the Elms. On the very morning of their arrival, in an obscure London church, Miss Raymond had given her hand to Captain Lawrence. He had consented to be baptized by an Anglican minister. Leila had insisted upon this concession from him, as she knew that otherwise her marriage would not be valid before God. She had got through the short period of necessary legal residence in the parish, by locating herself in humble apartments, where nobody knew her. She was in such a desperate state of mind, that to commit some strong rash act was a relief to her. She felt that self-respect commanded her to conquer her infatuation for one who had chosen a higher vocation, and she resolved to conquer it, if it cost her her reason or her life; but she went to work in the wrong way. She hoped by a violent wrench to subdue a mis-placed affection, instead of waiting until the grace of the sacraments and the influence of the great healer Time, should gradually restore her peace of mind. She came to a full conscious-ness of her sin and her error when it was too late.

After the nuptial ceremony, they set off for a pretty cottage, in the neighbourhood of Malvern, which had been bequeathed to Captain Lawrence by the aunt whose demise he had been so long expecting. He resolved to leave the army, and lead a quiet life. Leila wrote the news to 'Agnes. It was a great blow to the faithful heart of that young lady, and still more so to her father. But what was done could not be undone. The bride entreated that Agnes might be allowed to pay her a visit in the summer; but, of course, this was not permitted.

Sir Thomas took up his abode in one of our principal colleges, to complete the ecclesiastical studies which he had long ago commenced.

Charlotte and Agnes missed him dreadfully: but they were delightful companions to each other.

Jane began to form a fashionable circle of her own, which was quite apart from theirs. She had a remarkable faculty of throwing off grief, or any other strong mental impression, after a time. She possessed high spirits, when she was in a good temper; and these, in connection with her great musical talents, qualified her to shine in society. She devoted a great deal of time to dress and to parties. The heavy disappointment which she had suffered at Lucerne enraged and embittered her for a long while: but at last she sought consolation in the counsels of good Father Cuthbert.

CHAPTER VIII.

"Full oft the shadow of the weary earth
   Fell on her, as she sat alone ;
Yet not the less held she her solemn mirth,
   And intellectual throne."

UMMER was over, and the variegated tints of autumn began to show beautifully in the fairest of our London suburbs. A year has now passed since Miss Maxwell rejected Sir Julius Clare. That event had made no interruption in the friendship which his mother had always entertained for the young lady, since her childhood.

During the previous winter, when Charlotte was at Rome, the owner of Clarendon Park had seen a good deal of the fair Agnes. At first he

7

felt drawn to her, for her sister's sake ; but after a while, her own charming qualities asserted their natural influence, and he began to think that life might be very happy with such a wife. On the day of which we are going to speak, the garden at the Elms was still bright with dahlias and geraniums; and the afternoon sun shone cheerily on the blue dresses of Charlotte and Agnes, who were roaming about, arm in arm, lovelier themselves than all the flowers.

"I have a piece of news for you, dearest," began Agnes.

" Sir Julius has proposed—n'est-ce pas ?" inquired Charlotte—"I am so glad," she added.

"Are you quite sure, my own darling ?" asked Agnes, looking at her sister, with a mixture of admiration and wistfulness.

"Quite sure" — replied Charlotte, turning those hazel eyes of hers, which had never been crossed by a shadow of untruthfulness,— full in their soft lustre on her sister's face : "there are few things," she added, "which could have given me greater pleasure. I congratulate you, with all my heart. You have said yes, I trust "—and she pressed a fervent kiss on Agnes' glowing cheek.

"I have told him that he must wait till to-morrow for an answer; and he seemed to have no objection. We are all to dine at Lady Clare's to-morrow. Listen—Charlotte, I would not accept him, if I thought it would cost you the smallest pain."

"I believe it, my own beloved," said Charlotte; "but, independently of the delight of seeing you happy, I shall now have the satisfaction of feeling that I am innocent of having in any way spoiled the life of an excellent man, whom I esteem as a brother."

"And is it possible that you do not envy me?" said Agnes playfully, as they sat down on one of the garden benches, and each began to twine a wreath for her sister's hair.

"No indeed; I do not," said Charlotte heartily. "I do not wish to build a nest in this world. I like to be free to look forward to the Eternal years!"

7—2

"You are too good for this world—I almost expect to see you take wings and fly away. Do you know—I heard from Leila, this morning. She writes in the worst possible spirits, and says that she is ill, and dying to see either you or me."

" I will write and ask papa's permission to stay with her," said Charlotte ; "let that be my care—so nothing need trouble your present joy."

"O that is kind of you," said Agnes; "Leila is still very dear to me, though she disappointed us all so grievously."

The next day was one of unmingled happiness to all parties. Lady Clare received her future daughter-in-law with affection and pride. Mrs. Blunt and Jane were gratified: we will not attempt to describe the feelings of the persons who were the most deeply concerned.

Sir Thomas granted Charlotte's request, that she might be permitted to visit Mrs. Lawrence. The latter was in a most trying state. A low nervous fever hung about her, but the malady was chiefly mental. She knew that she had by her undutiful conduct inflicted a heavy blow upon the only man whom it was possible for her to love in the full sense of the term. She had done it partly in a spirit of pique and revenge; but the pain recoiled on herself, and repentance came too late. It came in a long fit of frenzied self-reproach, as soon as the fatal words were spoken which bound her to Captain Lawrence.

At first her husband was devoted to her, but when months passed away, and he found that she had no love to give him, that her heart contained nothing but the ashes of an extinguished volcano, he felt as any husband would feel, keenly disappointed. He had flattered himself that she would get over the girlish enthusiasm which he knew that she had felt for her guardian. The charms which had excited his admiration for her were gradually fading away. Her principal beauty had consisted in a subtle and ever varying change of expression. All this had now given place to a persistent gloom. Her temper, too, had lost its alternations of touching pathos and exuberant gaiety, and had become more and more irritable.

Charlotte was discouraged by none of these things. She devoted herself to the amusement of the invalid, and nursed her, when she required it, with the tenderest care. Clarendon Park was not more than a mile and a half from Laurel Cottage, and Father Austin—though he had a large village congregation to look after—found time to make an occasional visit to Miss Maxwell. He insisted that she should take a walk every day, for he saw that she was injuring her health by too close application to her charitable duties. Leila bitterly complained that she had no carriage. The fact was, her mother was so angry at her indiscreet and surreptitious marriage, that she withdrew a considerable portion of the very handsome allowance which her daughter had hitherto enjoyed. And the Captain's deceased aunt—though she had bequeathed Laurel Cottage to him—had left him nothing more. Mrs. Lawrence, whose tastes and habits, were luxurious, was sorely pained and mortified by these disappointments.

It was impossible for a thoughtful man like

her husband to be thrown for weeks into the society of such a woman as Miss Maxwell without being powerfully impressed. The charm of her gracefulness, the beauty of her mind, and the kindness of her disposition, found their way to his very soul, and excited in him that species of admiration, mingled with awe, which he might have conceived for an angel. There were certain fine elements in his nature which had never yet been brought to the light. Charlotte did him more good than fifty preachers could have done. She never obtruded her piety; but he saw that it was the spring of all her actions. He studied her profoundly; he watched her untiring patience in attending on her friend. He saw by the occasional quiver of the lip, and the changing colour, that it often cost her a hard struggle to keep down an impatient word. Sometimes she scolded Leila for her good, and pleased the Captain by the spirit which she displayed. Occasionally he tried to draw her out in arguments on religion; but her director advised her to keep clear of discussion.

So whenever he attempted this, she used to say playfully—

"Now, Captain Lawrence, I must refer you to a better theologian than I am. Father Austin will, I am sure, be happy to lend you books, and to answer your difficulties."

"You ladies are priest-ridden," he would say; "but I can't help having a respect for Father Austin, if one may judge of the tutor by his pupil."

And so it happened that Charlotte was a golden link between these two men. For her sake the Positivist put himself in connection with the Priest, who was clever enough to answer all his questions. But it was the power of Father Austin's holiness, more than the strength of his intellect, which subdued the unbeliever. It was his life of practical and heroic self-sacrifice which convinced Captain Lawrence of the divinity of the religion which he taught. Still, it seemed that there was one crowning grace wanting to complete the work.

Mrs. Lawrence's health was better, and it was time for Charlotte to return to Kensington. It was a fine afternoon in August, and she walked over to the park to say farewell to her old friend Father Austin. She found him in the garden, which adjoined the small Presbytery where he lived. He conducted her into the parlour, and kindly expressed his regret that she could not prolong her stay until Lady Clare's return to the country.

" You see, Father," she said, " Agnes wants me to be with her before the wedding."

" That is natural," said Father Austin; " well, I trust that she will be happy—indeed, I feel sure that she will."

" Have you any hope of Captain Lawrence's conversion ?" asked Miss Maxwell.

" The greatest hope," he replied.

" Oh, I am so glad," she exclaimed; " he owes everything to you."

" Far from it, my child; you have had more to do with his conversion, if it comes to pass, than I have. Let this encourage you for the future. The influence which a Catholic lady may bring to bear on society can hardly be over-estimated. Many, alas! throw away this precious talent, or render it negative by their worldly and inconsistent lives."

"But I have not given up the world, you know, Father."

"Nor do I wish that you should. The world is particularly in want of ladies who can both make themselves agreeable by their attractive qualities, and at the same time exercise a sanctifying influence over others. I consider that you have a great and important work to do for God in society, besides that to which you have devoted yourself among His poor. I intend to introduce you to a friend of mine, a Jesuit Father, and a very enlightened man, who will be of use to you in London, and to whom I advise you to give your entire confidence."

"But, Father," said Charlotte somewhat timidly, "I hope that you will continue to favour me with your direction."

"Yes, my child, as long as I can; but I may

be taken away, and I should like to think that I had left you in good hands."

Miss Maxwell caught his meaning; tears started to her eyes; she looked at him for a moment, and could not fail to remark the hectic colour of the cheek, and the unnatural brilliancy of the eye. She controlled her emotion, and said—

"Oh, Father, I am so sorry!"

"Don't be sorry for me, if our Lord calls me to my home."

"I am sorry for myself," she said.

"It will be no loss to you ultimately. The time has come when you require a better director than I have been. And Father Aloysius will do you more good than I could. Keep the gaze of the soul constantly fixed on God: human things may obscure that vision, but let the will—which is the superior part of the soul—go ever straight to God until the end."

Charlotte's heart was too full for words; she knelt for his blessing, and hastened away.

*　　*　　*　　*　　*

Two years have passed away, and Father Austin has gone to his eternal rest. In a paper which was discovered after his death, it appeared that he had made an offering of his life to God, to procure the conversion of Captain Lawrence. The sacrifice had been accepted, and the man of the world was now a fervent Catholic. Sir Thomas Maxwell has received the royal crown of the Priesthood. Leila had never recovered either her health or her peace of mind. To a character like hers, it was misery to be chained to a man whom she did not love, and agony unspeakable to have lost the friendship of him whom she had made the idol and the object of her life. She had written him two or three despairing letters, entreating his forgiveness for her conduct. He had sent her a message of pardon through Agnes, but he never wrote to her. Her mind became enveloped in the blackest gloom. She had staked her all on one cast, and she had lost. The fire of her soul and the energies of her mind had been misdirected. Her life was a wreck, and her state of nervous prostration was such that her friends were seriously alarmed.

"I shall be glad to die," she said one day to the young Lady Clare, who had come over from Clarendon Park to see her; "I hope to die in the peace of the Church, and that my spirit will be permitted to visit those who are dear to me. I do not mean that I shall appear to any one, but souls are sometimes allowed to have their Purgatory near certain altars, so I shall wander about, and frequent churches."

Agnes, who was now a happy wife and mother, could only entreat her not to talk so wildly. She could not administer consolation to one who steadily refused all comfort.

"There is one thing you can do for me," Leila recommenced; "I know that your father is on a visit to you. Ask him, implore him, Agnes, to come and see me once before I die."

Lady Clare started at this proposition, but replied in her own gentle sisterly way—

"The excitement might be bad for you, dear; I am afraid it would be."

"No; believe me it would strengthen me for my last hour."

"What would Captain Lawrence say ?"

"He is very good, he has consented; he knows that it is the last request that I shall ever make him."

"Well, I will speak to papa," said Lady Clare, and so she did.

The Reverend Sir Thomas Maxwell judged it expedient to grant the petition. He was himself anxious about the state of a soul who had been an object of so much solicitude to him in the past. Agnes arranged everything for the interview; and she left Leila alone on her couch in the drawing-room when she saw her father's approach from the window. She opened the door to admit him, and told him that she should remain within call.

The Priest's countenance wore an expression of pain as he looked on that youthful form and face, so changed, so blighted, in the summer of existence.

"May God bless you," he began. "Leila, I

know that your friends have been sincere with you; they have told you that your life is probably passing away. Have you prepared yourself, by a very sincere confession, for the change which is impending?"

"No, father, not yet; I could not do it. I could not collect my thoughts until I had seen you. But I would never have asked you to come," she added, with rising colour, "if I had not been almost on my death-bed."

"I know it," he replied; "and now, child, if ever any wish of mine was sacred to you, I entreat you, give all your thoughts to the eternity which is approaching. Think what you have to answer for. When I remember what a fair bud of promise you were a few short years ago, I tremble to think how you have wasted the talents and the advantages which our good God gave you. You have neglected the duties which a wife owes to her husband, and you might have had his soul to answer for."

"Indeed it is true," said Leila, beginning to cry. Her guardian had assumed a tone which was somewhat severe, because he saw that it was necessary to alarm her conscience.

"But," she continued, "my husband has forgiven me all my sins against him, and I hope that Almighty God will not be less merciful."

"I hope so too, but you must approach Him with sincere contrition."

"I will do anything you tell me—I will cry my eyes out," she exclaimed, too vehemently; for a fit of coughing came on, which exhausted her so much that Sir Thomas thought it necessary to summon his daughter, who did everything for her that the kindest care could devise. The next day Sir Thomas offered up the Holy Sacrifice in the chapel at Clarendon Park, on behalf of the wayward child who had once been so dear to him.

And his prayer was heard. It seemed as if strength, both mental and physical, was vouchsafed to Leila from that hour. Her recovery was slow but steady. Captain Lawrence had loved her in the past with a deep unrequited affection, until her long-continued coldness had diminished his devotion. Still, he could not bear the thought of losing her, and his kindness during her illness excited her gratitude. The strong counsels of her guardian sank deep into her heart, and brought forth fruit abundantly. She rose from her couch of sickness an altered person. Her beauty, though it had lost in vividness, had gained in refinement. There was a pensive air still lingering about her, which was inexpressibly touching. "Il faut souffrir, pour être belle," was exemplified in her case. Once more she asked her husband's pardon for her neglect of duty to him; his only answer was a pressure to his heart, which said more than words could have done.

She set herself to recover diligently all the ground that she had lost. She became regular and fervent in the frequentation of the Sacraments. She laid herself out for the good of the poor in her neighbourhood. By degrees, the playful grace which had characterized her of old returned, and she became once more an ornament to society.

8

When Sir Thomas Maxwell visited Worcestershire a twelvemonth afterwards, he found that Leila was the crown and glory of her husband.

"She is a plant of your training, and she does you credit," said Captain Lawrence, warmly, as his reverend guest was departing, after spending a happy day under his roof. "There are two things for which I thank God eminently—my wife, and the precious gift of Faith."

"God be praised!" was the rejoinder of Sir Thomas, as he fervently clasped the hand of the converted Positivist.

Miss Jane Maxwell was indebted for any prospect of salvation which she might have, to the prayers and good counsels of Father Cuthbert. He never lost sight of her; and though she was often immersed in worldliness, he held her to the outward observance of her religion. She had one or two offers of marriage, but they fell to the ground. Her faith was strong, but her practice was weak. She will probably be always a failure, the victim of a lost vocation.

Charlotte's life is so beautiful, so mixed up with the invisible and the divine, that when her last hour comes, though she will be regretted by a large circle of loving hearts in which her image is enshrined, death for her will have no terrors.

The exquisite union of affection and confidence which has always subsisted between herself and her father is likely to go on to the end.

The star of the Reverend Sir Thomas Maxwell is in the ascendant. His talents and virtues have found their natural sphere. His life is full of merits. His eloquence and his genius have been instrumental in drawing many souls to God.

THE END.

R. WASHBOURNE, PRINTER, 18 PATERNOSTER ROW, LONDON.